First U.S. edition 2011

Library of Congress Cataloging-in-Publication Data is available.

Library of Congress Catalog Card Number pending

ISBN 978-0-7636-5862-5

11 12 13 14 15 16 17 SCP 10 9 8 7 6 5 4 3 2 1

Printed in Humen, Dongguan, China

This book was typeset in Gill Sans.
The illustrations were done in watercolor and gouache.

Candlewick Press
99 Dover Street
Somerville, Massachusetts 02144

visit us at www.candlewick.com

How Do YOU Feel?

Anthony Browne

CANDLEWICK PRESS

How do you feel?

Well, sometimes I feel **bored** . . .

and sometimes I feel

lonely.

Sometimes I feel very happy . . .

and sometimes I feel *sad*.

Sometimes I feel ANGRY . . .

and sometimes I feel **guilty**.

Sometimes I feel curious . . .

THE MOST
DANGEROUS
POP-UP
EVER!

but then sometimes I'm **SURPRISED**!

I can feel **CONFIDENT** . . .

but I can also feel *shy*.

I can feel a bit worried . . .

but more often I feel REALLY **SILLY**!

Sometimes I feel very hungry . . .

and sometimes very **FULL**.

Right now, I feel a little sleepy.

How do
YOU
feel?

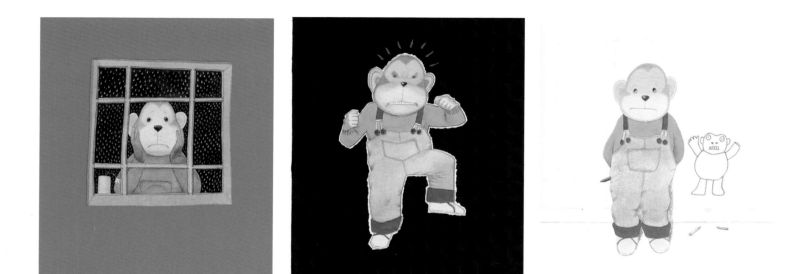

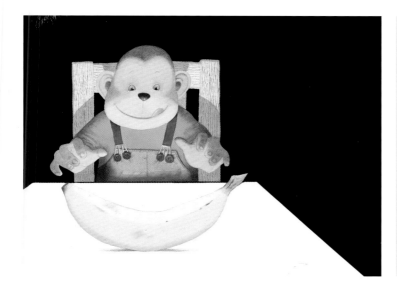